EDDIE GETS READY

FOR SCHOOL

DAVID Milgrim

Cartwheel
B·O·O·K·S·®

Scholastic

New York   Toronto   London   Auckland
Sydney   Mexico City   New Delhi   Hong Kong

For all the BIG kids who can do so much!

Library of Congress Cataloging-in-Publication Data

Milgrim, David.
Eddie gets ready for school / by David Milgrim. -- 1st ed.
p. cm.
Summary: As young Eddie goes through his checklist to get ready for school, his mother does not agree with all of his choices.
ISBN 978-0-545-27329-9 (hardcover (pob))
[1. Lists--Fiction. 2. Mothers and sons--Fiction.] I. Title.

PZ7.M5955Edd 2011
[E]--dc22

2010016779

ISBN 978-0-545-27329-9

10 9 8 7 6 5 4 3 2   11 12 13 14 15

Printed in Singapore 46
First edition, July 2011

A checklist for getting ready all by myself!
Feed dog
Feed Fish

☑ Have a
healthy
breakfast

☑ Feed
Mr. Chips

☑ Get
dressed

☑ Watch
cartoons

☑ Drink
root beer

Turn off
TV
this
instant

☑ Pour
out
root beer

☑ Really get
dressed

☑ Pack a
Snack

☑ Put cat
   in backpack

☑ Hug Mom